For my twin sister, Misun,
and all of the fond memories we share

Distributed in Canada by D&M Publishers, Inc.
Color separations by Chroma Graphics
Printed in May 2011 in China by Macmillan Production (Asia) Ltd.,
Kwun Tong, Kowloon, Hong Kong (supplier code 10)
Designed by Jay Colvin
First edition, 2011
1   2   3   4   5   6   7   8   9   10

www.fsgkidsbooks.com

Library of Congress Cataloging-in-Publication Data
Yum, Hyewon.
   The twins' blanket / Hyewon Yum. — 1st ed.
     p. cm.
   Summary: Two twin girls, who have always
shared everything, sleep in separate beds with their
own blankets for the first time.
   ISBN: 978-0-374-37972-8
   [1. Twins—Fiction.   2. Sisters—Fiction.
3. Blankets—Fiction.   4. Individuality—
Fiction.]   I. Title.

PZ7.Y89656Tw 2011
[E]—dc22

          2009046o922

the twins' blanket

Hyewon Yum

FRANCES FOSTER BOOKS

FARRAR STRAUS GIROUX

NEW YORK

We're look-alike twins.
That means we look like each other.

That means we share everything.

We share toys, clothes, and a room.

Once, we even shared Mommy's belly.

And we've shared the same blanket
ever since we were born.

That's what Mommy says.

But we are big girls now.
I'm already five.

I'm five, too. We're twin sisters, remember, silly? The blanket has gotten too small for both of us.

I think I should have this blanket.
Because I'm the big sister, and I can't sleep without it.

No, I think I should have it.

Because . . . well . . . I can't sleep without it, either.

And you're only three minutes older than me!

I am mad at my little sister!

Mad at me?

I am mad, too. You're so greedy.

Mommy says we should have separate beds now—
twin beds since we're big twin girls.

And she's going to make a new blanket for each of us.

We're buying new fabric for our blankets.
I pick yellow with flowers on it. Yellow is my favorite color.

Then we dry the fabric in the sun.
I think yellow is an excellent color for the blanket. Don't you?

The water tickles us. We laugh and laugh. It's so much fun!

Before she starts to sew,
Mommy lets us wash the fabric in the backyard.

I pick pink with birds and flowers. Pink is my favorite color.

No, pink is a much better color for everything!

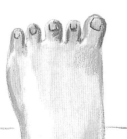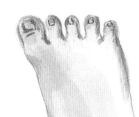

It takes a while—and a lot of sewing—to make two blankets.
I want Mommy to finish mine first.

No, mine first.
You always get to be first, and that's not fair!

Finally, they're finished.

Mine is so beautiful. Now I have my own blanket like a big girl.

I can't wait to sleep with it.

Mine is even more beautiful than yours. And it smells like sunshine.

We go to bed early, in our twin beds.
But I can't sleep.

Me neither.
My eyes are wide open in the dark.

I stretch my arm out. There's my little sister's hand.

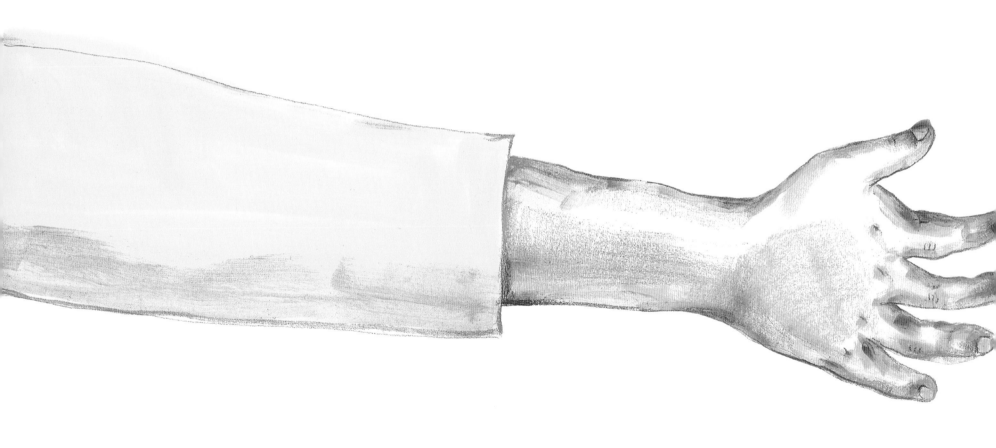

I hold my sister's hand tight. I think she is scared.

I was scared, but I feel better now.

Then we fall asleep
in our own beds,
with our own blankets,
for the very first time.